龍生九子

文／孟瑛如　　圖／林慧婷　　英文翻譯／吳侑達

光明正大

登場「龍」物

龍皇帝

龍皇后

龍老大

龍老五

龍老六

龍老七

龍老二

龍老三

龍老四

龍老八

龍老九

太子師

光明正大

在古老的動物帝國裡，龍皇帝握有至高無上的權力。他長得威武巨大，身上的鱗片都閃閃發光，嘴邊的鬍鬚都捲翹有型，剛猛的眉毛襯著炯炯有神的目光，益發顯得不怒自威！他總是睿智且機敏，將國家治理得極好，所有動物都順服於他。

龍皇帝唯一的苦惱，就是他的九個兒子個個都不像他，到底該由誰來繼承王位呢？

龍老大有著漂亮的黃色麟角，身材非常瘦小。這位擁有音樂細胞的龍子，自小熱愛音樂，喜歡玩各種琴，總是會走出動物帝國轄區，與人類在一起玩各種樂器。他不僅把漢族的胡琴拉得嚇嚇叫，就連少數民族彝族的龍頭月琴、白族的三弦琴，以及藏族的一些樂器，他都是箇中高手。

　　龍老二的眼睛像銅鈴那般大，擁有龍的身形，頭卻長得像豺狼。他的個性很剛烈，自小喜歡各種扭打戰鬥遊戲，總是可以看到他樂此不疲的在研究各種戰略攻守方法，滔滔不絕的與動物們討論各種歷史上重大戰役的勝負與攻防。

　　龍老三的身材修長，擁有雙翼。他喜歡冒險，總是希望自己
能像隻鳳凰，飛翔於天空。能夠站在一望無際的高處，迎著風
自在的看著美景是他最享受的事！
每當他外出旅遊回來，總愛站在皇
宮高高的屋簷上眺望著遠方。

龍老四有一個大大的頭配上寬寬的鼻梁，聲音非常洪亮，喜歡吼叫發洩情緒。他模仿廟裡銅鐘被撞擊的聲音總是維妙維肖，只要有他在的地方，一定熱鬧非凡，聲傳十里。

龍老五有著像獅子一般的雄偉鬃毛，個性上卻非常好靜，喜歡在檀香繚繞中盤腿打坐，有時甚至可以一整天不語不動！

龍老六個性慢條斯理，許多事情都會思考許久。他有著像烏龜一樣的寬背，最喜歡背重的東西，總是在身上疊滿各種東西，看看自己能背多重，挑戰自我極限！

龍老七有著像老虎一樣的斑紋跟頭部，非常喜歡辯論及追求真理，對於能斷是非的事特別感興趣，每天總能見到他在和不同的動物辯論，或是替動物們主持公道。

　龍老八和龍皇帝長得最像，但個性斯文，
總喜歡將身體盤繞在宮中的各種柱子上，靜
靜的看著大家活動。

龍老九的尾巴長得像魚，最喜歡吞下一大口水再去幫忙滅火，也喜歡到處灑水。動物帝國裡若有火災，他總是身先士卒，一馬當先到現場救火。皇宮中美麗的花圃與附近茂盛的森林，也都是他定期灑水照顧的對象。

　　動物帝國裡的太子師每天都在煩惱，不知該如何讓九位龍子學會治國。太子師常常提出應該要調高薪水並增聘其他協助教學的人力；因為龍太子們的程度與需求個個不同，異質性太高，他就算因材施教，常常使用最高超的「多層次教學技巧」與設計「多元化的區分式教材」，也還是覺得不知該拿這些外表和興趣差異甚大的龍子如何是好。

　　日子一天天的過去，龍皇帝苦惱不已，總是繞著宮殿來回踱步，嘴裡唸著：「我做錯了什麼事？怎麼會生出這些不成材的兒子們？」動物們也常議論紛紛，你一言我一語的討論龍皇帝的九個兒子該如何安排，因為關於各種治國人才的要求，九位龍子都很難獨自達成！

　　而且，從龍老大不被允許玩琴，需要大量吃東西，以求長得高大威猛，像個皇位繼承者，到龍老九被規定得在宮中學習各種治國理論，不能到處灑水、救火，九位龍子也越來越不快樂！

看著因為焦慮而開始啃咬自己鷹爪般的指甲，以致滲出血水的龍老二，以及開始會拔除自己鬃毛，以致脖子上有塊圓形禿的龍老五，龍皇后也很心急！她不斷的跟龍皇帝說：「孩子生來就是要做自己的！」「他們為什麼不能好好做自己？做最好的自己！」「王位為什麼一定要由他們繼承？為什麼不能選出其他既賢德又有才幹，而且對治理朝政有興趣的動物臣民來共同經營動物帝國？」

在龍皇后每天的勸說下，龍皇帝的想法慢慢開始改變了，

「對啊！孩子生來就是要做自己的。」

「孩子自己無法選擇要生在哪一家。他們除了興趣不在治國，每個孩子不都是健健康康、快快樂樂的嗎？」

「有健康的人未必有財富，有財富的人未必有快樂，有快樂的人未必有名望，我的孩子已經是健康、快樂、名望與財富兼具，我為什麼一定要他們去治國呢？」

「動物王國裡有許多賢德、有才幹、對治理國家也有興趣的動物臣民，為什麼不讓他們有機會做自己擅長的事，卻一定要強迫自己的孩子做既不拿手又不喜歡的事呢？」

「緊鄰的海底王國，海龍王採取選賢與能的民主方式治理國家，不也是挺好的嗎？」

　　龍皇帝念頭一轉，頓時豁然開朗，決定向隔鄰海底王國的民主制度借鏡，不再強迫自己的九個兒子非得要學習治國理念與實務，同時下詔：「龍生九子，各有不同，適性教之，可也！」並且規範全國教育制度都須因應每個孩子的個別需求，實施適性教育。「過往教養的失敗不是失敗，失敗只是讓我們轉一個方向，讓我們能夠過著屬於自己的『龍』生！」

光明正大

　　動物帝國的子民們因為龍皇帝的睿智仁政，開始注重起自己孩子的適性教育方式；同時，也因為採取選賢與能的民主方式來治理國家，每位子民都同樣有參與國政的機會，因而變得對國家更有向心力了！九位皇子從此恢復以往的快樂，做自己喜歡的事，各自用能貢獻自己所長於成長家園的方式，自在的生活著。

後世的動物子民為了感謝龍皇帝一家對國家的無私想法，以及在適性教育提倡上的重要啟發，紛紛將九位皇子的臉像與身形放在他們喜歡的物品上……

到了今日，我們會在漢族的胡琴，以及少數民族彝族的龍頭月琴、白族的三弦琴和藏族的一些樂器琴頭上，看到刻有龍老大頂著漂亮的麟角、揚頭張口的形象！

在各種軍用武器或是軍事基地裡，會看到龍老二瞪著銅鈴般大的眼睛，頂著龍身豺首，威風凜凜的注視著大家，要大家像他一樣，好好研究各種戰略攻守方法！

皇宮裡的殿角走獸或是屋頂的飛簷上，總是站著一隻長得像是龍跟鳳凰的揉合體，有時呈現展翅欲飛的形象，有時收斂翅膀靜靜站立，像在守護大家的平安——這就是最喜歡迎著風、望向遠方看美景的龍老三了！

在廟宇裡或樂器上，各種大小形式銅鐘提把上的方頭大鼻龍雕像，就是龍老四了，只要敲打或撞擊這些銅鐘，就能鳴聲遠揚！

長得跟獅子很像的龍老五，因為喜愛在煙霧繚繞處靜坐，所以在廟裡的香爐上，或是在雲霧環繞的深山古剎裡，常常會看到他的樣貌。偶爾在古董家具眠床的兩側欄杆上，也可以看到他的刻像。人們希望龍老五的好靜特質，可以幫助大家一夜好眠！

喜歡背重物，有著烏龜寬背的龍老六，力大到可以馱負三山五嶽，所以常常在房屋地基、表演台下方、石碑下、石柱下或是牆角裝飾上，看到他背著重物，像在鍛鍊身體般享受的模樣！

如果有機會參觀法院或是監獄，常常可以在正門的兩側看到長得像老虎的龍形象，這就是喜歡辯論與追求真理，好打官司和主持公道的龍老七了！

光明正大

龍老八的身形最像一條龍，後世常可見到他斯斯文文、安安
靜靜的盤在屋中圓柱或屋簷樑柱上的各種雕像，傾聽各種人事
物，笑看世間百態！

龍老九因為喜歡吞水滅火，也喜歡到處灑水，所以現在與我們日常生活密切相關的各種洗手台、浴室、自動澆花灑水器等的「水龍頭」，就是以他來取名的。消防車上也可以看到因為能夠幫助滅火救災，他得意微笑的樣子喔！

　　近十年來，有一千五百種以上的新興行業是以前的我們所想不到的，例如：手遊、虛擬實境、擬人化演算法等相關產業，或者中文系畢業的人進遊戲公司幫遊戲軟體寫對話劇本，甚至是訓練智慧機器人模擬人的思路歷程，學習溝通技巧，而不再如以往我們所想像的是當國文老師、小說家或是出版社編輯等。台灣的父母因過度寵愛孩子，常會想為孩子安排各種未來，並且堅信這是「為孩子好」，有時甚至希望子承父業。孩子的一生還如此長，充滿著無限的可能，他所處的世界更是在無限可能中變化著，所以除非是迷失了人生方向，不知道自己該做什麼，否則，我們為何一定要讓孩子重複別人的路呢？我們為何不能教孩子結合自己的天賦，做最好的自己呢？其實孩子跟我們生活在一起，耳濡目染之下，若不能對父母所從事的行業有興趣，恐怕他的興趣就不在這裡，而興趣能與工作結合，是一種值得擁有的人生福報！

　　繪本中龍皇帝認為自己給了孩子整個天下、一生的富貴，孩子卻像扶不起的阿斗，讓龍皇帝苦惱不已。難道為他們安排這樣的路不好嗎？但我們或許應該反問，父母所預備的路就一定好嗎？有的孩子要的其實是快樂，有的孩子要的是成就感，有的要的只是自在，而這些也許在父母所安排的路上是得不到的。

　　在教育現場曾看過許多例子，深覺常聽到的「放對位置就是人才，放錯位置就成為垃圾」這句話頗有道理。有幾個印象深刻的例子：一位總喜歡將東西撥到地上，聽物品碎裂聲的自閉症學生，因地利之便，母親懇求某鶯歌陶瓷廠老闆收容他學拉胚技術。沒想到第一天上班實習，他一進門便將展示架上的各種花瓶及陶藝作品一個一個慢慢撥到地上，享受各式各樣的清脆碎裂聲，半小時內讓母親賠了五萬多元。這個學生後來被轉換安排到資源回收場工作，他可以自由自在的操作機械，將所有回收寶特瓶壓縮成塊；在撞擊壓碎玻璃製品時，許多人討厭的噪音及燠熱的工作環境，對他來說完全不成問題，所以他總是準時到班，還常自願加班。他工作時，整個資源回收場如同他的大玩具間，臉上滿足的笑容令人難忘。

　　而另一位動作超級慢的發展性學習障礙生因不知對什麼事項有興趣，所以被送去學父母認為「比較好念」的中餐餐飲；但因中餐餐飲講求刀工俐落、大火快炒等基本功，實習時大廚覺得他簡直是「朽木不可雕也」，直接退訓。然而後來轉到食品加工行業後，他如樹懶般的慢功夫反而成為特色。還記得他微笑的說：「醃梅子的時候最快樂，因為梅子不會催我快！」；腦性麻痺學生結合每天一定要做的物理及職能訓練動作揉麵團做麵包，因為要做到規定的物理職能動作訓練量，結合每個做麵包的流程，他做出來的麵包外脆內軟，美味可口極了；也曾遇過明知孩子鑑定後為注意力缺陷過動症伴隨學習困難問題，卻仍一心嚮往孩子成為醫生的爸媽，因父母認為孩子自小對昆蟲獨角仙有興趣，一定適合讀生物相關的第三類組，說不定就可以幸運考上醫科。這孩子在經過一番家庭革命後選念高職汽修科，還記得當時我勸他父母的話是：「只是醫治車子跟醫治人的差別，而且日後修理汽車或機器人說不定比醫人要更困難呢！因汽車設備內容每年在變，但人體構造不會變！」他的父母應該很喜歡這種說法，所以終於首肯讓我們將兒子安置到高職汽修科；也有家長在身障學生升學安置會議會場要我們不要管孩子了，也不願意讓孩子升學，因為父母覺得升學沒有用，他們以後會留另一個博士兒子養他——也就是每個月可收10萬元租金，形同大學教授月收入的超商店面。我要父母先確認在兒子成年時超商經營仍是主流，同時他的兒子能守得住這間店面才可以養自己一輩子，更何況讓孩子依興趣多個一技之長有什麼壞處呢？父母才終於轉念。

在與家長接觸的過程中，總覺得心焦的父母太多，喜歡比較的父母太多；然而，願意好好花時間在孩子身上，在孩子學習任性做自己的過程中，扮演他們人生最重要的引導者，引導他們能做最好的自己的韌性者少。社會上所謂的「好」，定義其實是很多元、很抽象的，不一定是固定的樣子與標準，才能當我們的好孩子。

如果我們可以同意成功的定義因人而異的觀點，便能接受成功有許多不同的面貌與方向，也或許更能體會所謂「成功是得到自己想要的，但幸福卻是喜歡自己得到的」。教會孩子與自己競爭、與他人合作的生活態度，也許是我們能給他們的珍貴教養資產之一。繪本中的龍皇帝最終能明白「適性教育」這個觀點，而不再煩憂龍生九子，皆不肖父。此外，本繪本將故事中的龍皇帝、龍皇后、太子師及九位龍子的圖像另製成貼紙，每張貼紙圖像都各自展示著他們的專長與創意，建議在孩子表達出自己對未來的期許、努力過好每一天、享受或許微小卻堅定的進步時，能給予一枚貼紙做鼓勵！也期待能以這本《龍生九子》的繪本，與所有願意協助孩子做最好的自己之家長及教師共勉！

The Dragon Emperor and His Nine Dragon Sons

Written by Ying-Ru Meng ／ Illustrated by Hui-Ting Lin ／ Translated by Arik Wu

Characters

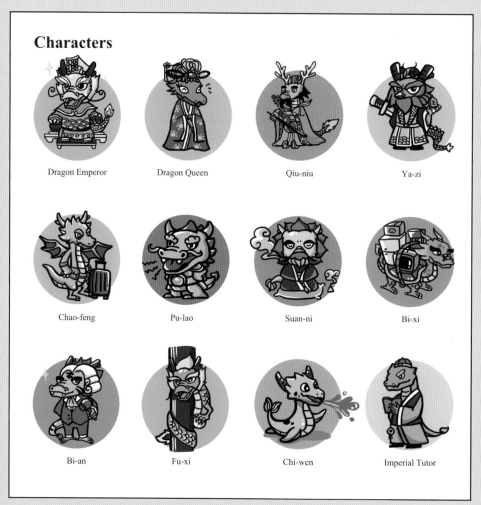

Dragon Emperor   Dragon Queen   Qiu-niu   Ya-zi

Chao-feng   Pu-lao   Suan-ni   Bi-xi

Bi-an   Fu-xi   Chi-wen   Imperial Tutor

Note: For the sake of clarity, all characters in the English version use their real names instead of code names or nicknames such as 龍老大 (the first dragon son) and 龍老二 (the second dragon son). For more detailed information, visit https://zh.wikipedia.org/wiki/龍生九子.

Once upon a time, there was an empire ruled by animals. The emperor was a gigantic, formidable-looking dragon. Not only did he have amazingly splendid scales and curly, stylish beard, but he also had a natural majesty in him. As an extraordinarily wise and resourceful king, he ruled his empire well. Not one animal dared to challenge his will.

Yet there was one thing worrying him. He had nine sons, but none of them had grown into a real dragon like he was. Who could succeed him as emperor?

Qiu-niu, the eldest son, was a relatively small dragon with beautiful yellow horns. He fell in love with music the moment he was born, and he was very good at playing qins[1]. Whenever possible, he would travel beyond the empire's territory to enjoy playing music with humans from other areas. Over time, he became an expert not only in Han people's huqins, but also in Yi people's yueqins, Bai people's sanxians[2], and some Tibetan musical instruments.

Note: 1. qin: A Chinese musical instrument.
2. sanxian: A Chinese lute.

Ya-zi, the second son, had the head of a jackal and the body of a dragon. His eyes were as big as brass bells. He was fierce, bellicose, and grew up having an interest in wrestling and all sorts of military tactics and strategies. He was always seen discussing with other animals about the tactics used in some major battles in history.

Chao-feng, the third son, had a pair of wings and a slender figure. He was fond of going on adventures, and had always wished he could be like a phoenix, flying in the sky and traveling around the world. Standing on a high place and enjoying beautiful scenery in the distance was his favorite thing to do. Therefore, whenever he returned from his travels, he always went onto the palace's rooftop and started looking into the distance.

Pu-lao, the fourth son, had a loud voice and a huge head with big nostrils. He loved giving vent to his emotions through roaring and was an expert in imitating the sound of temple bells. Whenever he was present, the atmosphere would be boisterous and loud, and even animals who were living in places far away could hear his voice!

Suan-ni, the fifth son, had lion-like, majestic mane, but was actually more of the quite type. He loved meditating in a quiet room filled with incense. Sometimes he could even remain seated for a whole day without talking or moving.

Bi-xi, the sixth son, was a slower thinker. Carrying heavy things on his turtle-shell resembling back was his favorite thing to do. Therefore, he always carried a variety of things on his back, just to see how much weight he could possibly bear!

Bi-an, the seventh son, had stripes on his face and looked just like a tiger. He was born a debater and was always in pursuit of truth and justice. Therefore, he often engaged in debates with other animals and gave justice to where justice belonged!

Fu-xi, the eighth son, resembled the dragon emperor the most. Unlike his father, however, he had a rather graceful and gentle temperament. He was more interested in winding his body around the pillars in the palace and observing others in stillness and silence than engaging in activities with other animals.

Chi-wen, the youngest son, loved putting out fires and watering plants with water he just swallowed. Whenever a fire broke out, he was always the first one to arrive at the scene. Apart from that, the beautiful gardens in the palace and the flourishing forests in neighboring areas were all cultivated by him!

Complaints from the tutor who taught the nine dragon princes were pretty common. He complained almost every day that he did not quite know how to teach them to govern an empire, as each of them required a completely different pedagogy. None of the study plans, multilevel curriculums, and differentiated instruction strategies he had developed worked out so far for these dragon sons of different sizes and learners' motivation. Therefore, he was always saying that there should be a raise in his salary and that the dragon emperor should hire more tutors to assist him in carrying out those pedagogies.

As days went by, the dragon emperor became more and more agitated. He could not help speed walking around the palace back and forth, mumbling to himself: "What have I done wrong? Why is every one of my children so useless?"

Animals in the empire were also worried. They did not know what to do with the nine dragon princes, since every one of them did not seem capable enough to shoulder the responsibility of running this empire. The dragon emperor then decided to resort to drastic measures. Qiu-niu was not allowed to play qins anymore; instead, he needed to spend his time on eating a lot of foods, so that he could grow as gigantic and majestic as a crown prince was supposed to be. Also, Chi-wen was now asked to study politics all the time and was prohibited from putting out fires around the empire as he pleased.

As each day passed, the nine dragon sons became more and more unhappy.

Ya-zi started biting his eagle-like claws out of anxiety, so hard that they bled. A bald patch appeared in Suan-ni's scalp because he could not help plucking his mane. The dragon queen, therefore, was extremely worried. "Children are born to be themselves! Why can't our sons just be who they want to be?" "Let them be the best of themselves! Why do they need to shoulder such responsibility?" "Why don't you look for animals that are capable and interested enough to collaborate in governing our empire?" she said to the dragon emperor.

The dragon emperor eventually gave in to the queen's daily grumbles, and decided to look at things from a different perspective. "You're right. Our sons have the right to be who they want to be."

"They can't choose their family. Indeed, none of them wants to rule this empire, but does it really matter? As long as they are healthy and happy, it is good enough already."

"Health doesn't guarantee wealth, wealth doesn't guarantee happiness, and happiness doesn't guarantee fame. But now all my children are healthy, wealthy, happy, and famous, what is the point of having to force them to do things they don't like?"

"There are many animals who are wise and capable of running this empire. If they are interested, why don't I give them a chance to do it and allow my children to do what really intrigues them and what they are really capable of doing?"

"Isn't the nearby Underwater Kingdom a democracy? It does not seem to be a bad political system, I think."

Things were all sorted out for the dragon emperor. He made up his mind to learn from the neighboring democratic Underwater Kingdom, and no longer forced his children to study politics or to learn how to govern the empire.

In addition, the dragon emperor also sent out an edict to all the animals in the empire, saying, "I am blessed with nine sons. Though it is true that none of them has grown into a real dragon, individualized instructions can still help them succeed." He demanded that the empire's education system should use individualized instruction to meet students' varied needs and to better develop their potential. "Reflecting on our past failures is a

way for us to move toward the right direction. Now I understand how important it is to live a life that is uniquely mine!" he wrote at the end of his edict.

Deeply impressed by the dragon emperor's words of wisdom, animals in the empire began to realize how crucial it is to have their children receive the kind of education that best fits them. Additionally, since the empire had transformed into a democracy, every animal had the opportunity to participate in public affairs, and thus fostering a stronger sense of community among themselves.

The nine dragon princes also seemed to be back to their normal selves. They were once again enjoying their lives to the fullest, and continued contributing their special talents to the empire.

Fast-forward to the present. People nowadays like to embed the images of the nine dragon sons in the things they loved, as a way to commemorate the imperial family's selfless contributions to the empire and the popularity of individualized instruction.

Nowadays, People can see the image of Qiu-niu and his beautiful horns on Han people's huqins, Yi people's yueqins, Bai people's sanxians, and some Tibetan musical instruments.

As for Ya-zi, his image can be seen on a variety of weapons and buildings in military bases today. With eyes as big as brass bells, it seems as though he was casting intimidating gazes at people all the time, telling them to study military strategies and tactics as hard as he did.

What about Chao-feng, hybrid of dragon and phoenix? His statuettes can be seen on the ridge lines and the rooftops of palaces. Sometimes spreading his wings as if he was about to soar into the sky, and sometimes folding them to his sides and quietly looking into the distance, ready to warn people of any nearing threats.

Moving on to Pu-lao. With a huge, square-shaped head and huge nostrils, Pu-lao's statuettes can now be seen on the handles of temple bells and musical instruments. It is his job to have the sounds of these bells and instruments travel as farther as can be!

Where is Suan-ni, the lion-like dragon who loved meditating in silence? His image can be seen on the side railings of antique furniture or in temples located in foggy and misty mountains. Helping people to sleep tight at night is his job!

What about Bi-xi, the dragon who loved carrying heavy things on his back and was strong enough to shoulder even the heaviest mountains? Where is he right now? His sculptures can not only be found at building foundations, but also at the bottom of steles, tablets, and pillars. With heavy things on his back, it seems as if he was doing workouts joyfully!

If people visit courthouses or prisons, they can often see statues of a tiger-like creature standing on both sides of the entrances. Without a doubt, it is Bi-an, the dragon who was always settling disputes and in pursuit of justice!

What about Fu-xi? Where is this graceful and gentle dragon right now?

His sculptures can often be seen resting quietly on pillars and beams in different kinds of houses, as if observing and contemplating on everything around him!

As for Chi-wen, the youngest dragon son, his passion for putting out fires and watering plants has inspired the word "shui-long-tou" (literally the head of a water dragon), the Chinese term for "faucet." Also, his proud, smiley face can often be seen on fire engines rushing to fire scenes!